KU-441-801

ANIMAL ARK

Reindeer Recovery

Lucy Daniels

STORY ONE:
The Christmas
Extravaganza

STORY TWO:
Reindeer Rescue

STORY ONE:
The Christmas Extravaganza

CHAPTER ONE

"Look at this!" Amelia said, holding up a tiny golden reindeer for Sam to see. She turned it in her hand, making it sparkle under the bright lights of the treatment room at Animal Ark. "It's one of Father Christmas's reindeer!"

Amelia hung the decoration on the

little Christmas tree beside Mr Hope's desk, nestling it between a shiny red bauble and a shimmering icicle.

Sam delved into the cardboard box on the treatment table, making the paper inside rustle. "Here's another one!" he said, drawing out a reindeer covered in red glitter. He hooked it on to a low branch beside a silver star.

"You two are doing a fantastic job," Mr Hope said, coming

back into the room with an armful
of tinsel. "I'm really starting to feel
Christmassy now! Are you all ready for
the Extravaganza next Sunday?"

Amelia grinned and nodded. "My
costume's nearly done!" she said. "Mrs
Cranbourne's just making the final
adjustments."

"We're both going to be elves in the
parade," Sam said proudly. "We get to
throw sweets into the crowd."

Amelia felt a thrill of excitement as she
thought of the Extravaganza. The school
choir was going be there, along with
most of her class. *I can't wait!*

"Caleb and Izzy are dressing up too,"

Sam told Mr Hope. "They're in charge of collecting donations. All the money is going to a guide dog charity, so we're hoping to make as much as possible."

Mr Hope smiled. "Well, if you put as much energy into the parade as you do into helping out at the surgery, it's bound to be a big success. Do you know who's going to play Father Christmas?" he asked. Then, tucking his thumbs into imaginary braces, he let out a deep "Ho, ho, ho!"

Amelia giggled. With his short brown hair and dark-rimmed spectacles, Mr Hope couldn't have looked less like Father Christmas. "No one's told us

who's playing him yet," she said.

Sam frowned slightly. "It's funny we don't know. We're going to be his elves, after all!"

Mr Hope glanced up at the clock. "Well, maybe I can help you there. Mrs Cranbourne and Miss Fizz are due for an appointment shortly. You can ask Mrs Cranbourne – she must know, since she's the one organising everything."

The intercom on Mr Hope's desk bleeped. "That will be her now!" he said, picking up the receiver. "Send her through," Mr Hope told Julia, the receptionist.

The door to the treatment room

opened, and Mrs Cranbourne came in holding an animal carrier. The look of worry on the elderly lady's face sent a jolt of alarm through Amelia. *I hope Miss Fizz is all right!* Amelia could just make out the little cat's tortoiseshell fur through the carrier bars.

"So, how can I help?" Mr Hope asked.

Mrs Cranbourne shook her head,

wringing her hands. "Miss Fizz wouldn't eat her breakfast this morning. She's got a horrible cough and it's getting worse."

Along with her worry for Miss Fizz, Amelia felt a rush of sympathy for Mrs Cranbourne. She looked so upset! Amelia had once been scared of Mrs Cranbourne, but that was before she'd realised that the old lady had been lonely ever since her previous cat had passed away. Adopting Miss Fizz had changed Mrs Cranbourne completely.

Mr Hope unclipped the lid of the animal carrier. "Out you come then, Miss Fizz," he said, scooping the young cat up with one hand. Miss Fizz was

sister to Amelia's own cat, Star. Usually, she greeted Amelia with a loud miaow whenever she passed Mrs Cranbourne's house, and curled about her legs, asking to be petted. But now all the little cat could manage was a half-hearted mew. Her fur looked dull and her green eyes were half-closed and gummed up at the corners. When Mr Hope set her down, she sat hunched on the table with her ears flicked back, looking truly fed up.

"Let me check you over, then," said Mr Hope, scratching the little tortoiseshell cat behind the ears. Miss Fizz lifted her chin, screwed up her eyes and let out a snotty-sounding sneeze.

"Bless you!" Mr Hope said. After putting on a pair of blue gloves, he gently examined Miss Fizz. First, he took her temperature, then he inspected her eyes with a light. Finally, he listened to the cat's chest with a stethoscope for a long, tense minute. Amelia's own chest tightened with worry as the crackling sound of Miss Fizz's breathing filled the silence. She glanced up to see Sam biting his lip.

"Hmm," Mr Hope said, straightening. "She does have quite a wheeze, and there's

definitely some dullness in her chest. Her temperature is a little high, too. I think she may have pneumonia."

"Pneumonia! But that's terrible!" Mrs Cranbourne said, her worried eyes looking huge behind her glasses.

"It's actually fairly common in cats," Mr Hope said. "And we've caught it early so it should be easy to treat. Does Miss Fizz play outside a lot?"

"Yes, all the time!" Mrs Cranbourne told him. "Normally she has so much energy. She's up and down trees and fences most of the day, and only really comes in at night."

"Well, she'll have to stay indoors for

a bit now," Mr Hope said. "She's still very young and it's been frosty recently, so she'll be a bit more vulnerable than usual. She probably caught a cold, and it's turned into a bacterial infection. Once she's better, she can go back outdoors. With luck, she'll be better before Christmas."

Amelia saw a pink flush of relief spread over Mrs Cranbourne's face, and felt her own tense muscles relax. *Christmas is only a couple of weeks away, so Miss Fizz can't be that ill!*

"I'll give her an injection of antibiotics now," said Mr Hope. "You can give her another dose tomorrow, and by then she should have perked up a bit. But if she gets worse, or if you're worried, bring her back. Amelia, can you hold Miss Fizz while I give her the jab?"

Mrs Cranbourne set her cat down again, and Amelia gently put a hand on either side of Miss Fizz's body. Mr Hope lifted the loose skin on the scruff of Miss Fizz's neck, and quickly gave the injection. The little cat didn't even flinch.

"Good girl," Amelia said, stroking Miss Fizz. Then she lifted the little cat back into the carrier, where she quickly settled down on to her blanket.

"Thank you so much!" Mrs Cranbourne said again, picking up the carrier to leave. But as Sam opened the door for her, Amelia suddenly remembered something.

"Ooh! Before you go, we've all been wondering who is going to play Father Christmas in the parade," she said.

Mrs Cranbourne pursed her lips into a mysterious smile that made her eyes twinkle. "I couldn't possibly tell you," she said. "It's a secret!"

CHAPTER TWO

Amelia smiled, drawing in a long breath of frosty air scented with pine needles and spices. Christmas music blared from every shop, and people bundled in warm coats and scarves bustled about the square. A long line of parents with children waited outside a Santa's Grotto

covered in glittering fake snow.

Amelia put her hand in her pocket and felt her heavy purse, filled with coins. "Where should we go first?" she asked Sam. Amelia's dad had brought them both Christmas shopping in York and had arranged to meet them back at the grotto later.

"Hmm," Sam said, gazing about. "I still need to get something for my mum. Maybe we should look at the stalls?"

"Good idea!" Amelia said. They struck off down a busy side street, passing rows of wooden huts filled with all the colours and smells of Christmas. Clouds of steam wafted from displays of spicy sausages and pans of hot chocolate and mulled wine. A stall with a beautiful display of candles caught Amelia's eye.

"These are pretty," she said. The candles had been dipped in coloured wax and carved to look like flowers.

Sam picked out a box of floating candles shaped like daffodils.

"Daffodils are Mum's favourite flower," he said, tucking them in his bag after he'd paid.

Next, they found a stall selling delicious-looking handmade chocolates and fudge. Amelia chose vanilla fudge for her mum and chocolate for her dad, then she and Sam clubbed together to buy a box of iced ginger biscuits for Mr and Mrs Hope.

"Hey! Look at this!" Sam said, beckoning Amelia excitedly towards the next stall. It only sold pet treats and toys. Sam quickly found a rope chew-toy for his Westie, Mac, while Amelia chose a felt mouse with a bell inside for Star.

The only person Amelia still needed to buy a present for was Sam. She'd been scratching her head for weeks, trying to think of something special. Amelia checked her watch. *Ten minutes until we meet Dad … Maybe I'll get an idea of what Sam would like if we go to a toy shop.*

Amelia steered Sam through the crowds towards a big toy shop she'd often

27

visited with her parents when they had all lived together in York.

Inside, Amelia immediately noticed a huge dolls' house. It was three storeys high, in the style of a Victorian townhouse with pointed gables. The front stood open, showing tiny furniture inside, and a doll family sat around a table set for Christmas dinner. In front of the dolls' house stood a little girl with chestnut bunches, tugging on the hand of a big, bald man with broad shoulders.

"Look! There's even a teeny cot for the baby!" the girl said, pointing.

"It's overpriced plastic, if you ask me!" the big man said. Amelia and Sam both recognised his grumpy voice at the same moment and exchanged a look of surprise.

"Mr Ferguson!" Sam said.

The bald-headed man often stayed at the bed and breakfast run by Sam's parents when he was working in Welford, but now Amelia hardly recognised him. Instead of his usual biking leathers Mr Ferguson had on a knitted Christmas

jumper covered in snowmen. As he turned, his bearded face broke into a smile.

"Hello, you two!" He tipped his head towards the little girl. "This is my niece, Paloma. She lives in Walton. I've brought her to town to see the Christmas lights. Paloma, meet Sam and Amelia."

Paloma smiled up at them, her brown eyes shining and her cheeks pink from the warmth of the shop.

"Uncle Bill

is coming to our house for Christmas dinner," Paloma said. "Only he never stays long, because he's too big to fit in our house!"

"Cheeky!" Mr Ferguson said, pretending to frown. "What she means is that there's no spare bedroom."

"Are you coming to the Welford Christmas Extravaganza?" Amelia asked. "We're going to be elves in the parade and we're giving out free sweets. And there's going to be carols and face painting and a tombola."

"Face painting!" Paloma said, jumping up and down. She tugged her uncle's arm. "Can we go, Uncle Bill? Please!"

31

"All that noise and fuss?" Mr Ferguson said, frowning. "No, thank you. You can go if you want, but your parents will have to take you. Now, if you're done staring at that dolls' house, shall we go and get some hot chocolate?"

"With cream on top?" Paloma asked eagerly.

"We'd better go too," Sam told Amelia. "It's almost time to meet your dad."

Outside the toyshop, Amelia and Sam waved goodbye to Mr Ferguson and Paloma, and headed back through the crowded streets. *I just don't know what to buy Sam for Christmas,* Amelia thought as they walked past people holding bags of

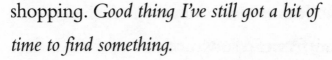

shopping. *Good thing I've still got a bit of time to find something.*

When they reached the square, they found it busier than ever. Amelia's heart gave a skip of excitement as she spotted why. Beside Santa's Grotto, a pen had been set up, and over the heads of the gathered children, she could just make out antlers.

"Reindeer!" Sam said. "Awesome!"

Amelia glanced towards the agreed meeting place, but her dad hadn't arrived yet. "Shall we take a closer look?" she asked Sam.

They eased their way through the crowd of children to a pen with a pair of reindeer inside. When they reached the front, Amelia saw that one of the reindeer had pushed his nose through the bars. A little boy, no older than two, reached out and gently stroked the reindeer's coat with his pudgy fingers. The sight gave Amelia an idea. She turned to Sam, almost bursting with excitement.

"Do you think we could get real reindeer to appear at the Extravaganza?" she asked him.

"Oh! That would be amazing!" said Sam. "But won't they be very busy at Christmas?"

"Well, there's no harm in asking," Amelia said. A dark-haired man wearing

a leather apron and wellies stood inside the pen with the reindeer. Amelia and Sam skirted around the children and waved to get his attention.

"How can I help?" the man asked, meeting them at the fence. He looked about the same age as Amelia's dad. He had tanned, weathered skin and friendly brown eyes, surrounded by deep smile lines.

"Hello," Amelia said. "Our village is holding a Christmas Extravaganza next weekend. There's going to be a big parade with a Father Christmas. It's for charity, and we were wondering if your reindeer might be able to come and walk in the parade too."

"It's on Sunday," Sam added. "In Welford."

The man tipped his head thoughtfully. "We're back here Wednesday and Friday," he said, "but Sunday is free. Twinkle and Jingle have done a few Christmas parades already this year. We've got a sleigh for them too, if you're interested. It has wheels as well as runners for when there's no snow."

"Oh! That sounds amazing!" Amelia said.

"We'll need to ask Mrs Cranbourne, who's organising everything," Sam said. "But I bet she'll say yes!"

"Why don't you take this to show her," said the man, handing them a card with the name *John Brathen* printed on it. "If

you want to book Twinkle and Jingle, just give me a call."

"Thank you!" Amelia could hardly hold in her excitement. She wanted to jump up and down. *I can't believe we might actually have real reindeer for the Christmas Extravaganza!*

CHAPTER THREE

The next day, Amelia sat beside the
flickering fire, half watching as her gran
ran through a series of stretches on her
Pilates mat. The click of Amelia's knitting
needles mingled with the crackle of the
flames and Amelia could hear Christmas
music playing softly in the kitchen where

her mum was cooking a Sunday roast.
With the sun setting pink and mauve
through the window, and the smell of
roasting potatoes in the air, the cottage
felt cosier than ever.

"You're doing really well there," Gran
said, looking over her shoulder at Amelia.

"Thanks, Gran," Amelia said. "I think
I'm starting to get the hang of it."

After only her first knitting lesson,
Amelia already had a good fifteen
centimetres of fairly neat stitches –
the start of a red woollen blanket she
planned to donate to Animal Ark.

A sudden tug at her needle broke her
rhythm. Amelia looked down to see Star
rolling on her back, with all four paws
buried deep into her ball of wool.

Amelia giggled. "You're not helping,
Star!" She set down
her knitting and
carefully unpicked
Star's claws from
her yarn, but as
soon as she'd freed

one paw, the little cat latched straight on to the sleeve of Amelia's jumper.

"You're like Velcro!" Amelia said. She'd just managed to unhook Star's claws again when the doorbell rang.

"I'll get it," Amelia said to her gran,

heading out to the hall with Star at her heels. She opened the door to find Mrs Cranbourne beaming at her, holding out a bright red and green outfit.

"I've finished the last nips and tucks,"

44

Mrs Cranbourne said. "Your elf costume is ready for next weekend."

"Thank you!" Amelia said, taking the outfit. "I've got something for you as well." She picked up the card Mr Brathen had given her from the hall table. "Sam and I met a reindeer handler in York yesterday. He has a sleigh and a pair of reindeer called Twinkle and Jingle. We wondered if you might want to book them for the parade."

"What a lovely idea!" Mrs Cranbourne said. "A sleigh for Father Christmas! That would be just the thing to attract an even bigger crowd – which means more money for the guide dog charity."

Hearing Mrs Cranbourne mention Father Christmas made Amelia more curious than ever. "Do you think we should tell Santa that he's going to have real reindeer?" she asked, smiling as innocently as she could. "I'll do it, if you like?"

"Will you indeed?" Mrs Cranbourne said, arching an eyebrow. "I don't see how, since I'm not going to tell you who he is."

Amelia laughed. "It was worth a try," she said. "How is Miss Fizz doing?"

Mrs Cranbourne's face softened into a smile. "She's so much brighter already. She even had some chicken for breakfast.

46

Now I'd better get along. I don't want
to let any more cold air into your house.
And thank you for this," she said, holding
up Mr Brathen's card.

Looking at her finished costume,
Amelia scooped up Star and gave her a
little squeeze. *Only a week to go until the
Extravaganza!*

The next school week flew by. On
Saturday, Sam and Amelia had a riding
lesson at Welford Stables. Afterwards,
they stood waiting with their instructor,
Fran, their breath hanging like mist in
the wintry morning air. Fran had kindly

agreed to put Mr Brathen's reindeer up for the night before the parade, and she'd invited Sam and Amelia to stay and meet them.

A thick frost covered everything with sharp crystals of ice, and the ground crunched under Amelia's boots as she stamped her feet to keep warm. Sam tucked his hands into his coat pockets.

"Why don't you two say hello to Walnut and Ginger while you're waiting?" Fran called from inside the stable she was mucking out. "Walnut's so much calmer now, thanks to you."

"It's thanks to Ginger, really," Amelia said, crossing to Walnut's stable with Sam.

But, as Walnut and Ginger came happily to meet them at the stable door, tails swishing and eyes bright with interest, Amelia felt a warm glow of pride that she'd been able to help. Walnut, Fran's young horse, had been so nervous that Fran almost had to give up riding him.

He would buck and bolt all the time.
But since Amelia worked out that being
around Ginger, a sturdy little Shetland
pony, made the bigger horse feel calm,
Walnut was much more relaxed. Fran
could even enter Walnut in cross-country
competitions.

While Sam held his knuckles out for
Walnut to sniff, Amelia stroked Ginger's
shaggy golden mane. The pony lifted his
soft nose to nuzzle her hand, and looking
into Ginger's big, gentle eyes, Amelia felt
a quiet peacefulness steal over her. *Ginger
could make anyone calm!*

At that moment, the crunch of tyres
on gravel sent a thrill of anticipation

through Amelia. She glanced over to see a jeep pulling a horsebox turn into the stables's drive.

"They've arrived!" she cried. Sam and Amelia hurried towards the courtyard's metal gate, and opened it wide to let the jeep in.

"Hello," Mr Brathen said, greeting Sam and Amelia with a big smile as he got out of his car. Then he unhitched his horsebox and let down its metal ramp, whistling a Christmas tune while he worked.

"Come on then, my lovelies," Mr Brathen said, beckoning to the reindeer inside. One of the deer, a small, caramel-coloured animal with velvety antlers, stepped on to the ramp and then down into the courtyard, her eyes bright as she gazed about.

Mr Brathen gave the reindeer a hearty pat on the rump. "Good girl, Twinkle," he said. But as he beckoned for his second reindeer, Jingle, Mr Brathen's eyebrows knitted together with concern. Amelia gazed into the shadows of the horsebox to see Jingle standing with his head hung low. And in the still morning air, she could just make out a crackling wheeze as the animal breathed.

"Jingle?" Mr Brathen said. "What's up, eh?" Jingle slowly lifted his head, then

let it fall again, but not before Amelia
noticed that he had a runny nose.

She felt a pang of alarm. *Oh no …
Jingle looks sick!*

CHAPTER FOUR

Amelia watched anxiously as Mr
Brathen took hold of Jingle's red leather
halter and led him slowly down the ramp
and out into the open. Sam rested a
calming hand on Twinkle's flank.

"I don't know what can be wrong with
him," Mr Brathen said, running a hand

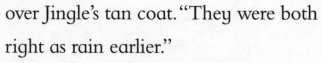

over Jingle's tan coat. "They were both right as rain earlier."

The sick reindeer stood stiffly with his nose almost touching the ground, as if his antlers were too heavy to lift. Apart from a brief flick of one ear, he didn't move, and Amelia could clearly hear the crackle of his chest now. The sound reminded her of Miss Fizz.

"His chest is quite noisy," she said. "Do you think Jingle might have pneumonia?"

"Maybe we should call the Hopes?" said Sam.

"The Hopes are our local vets," Fran told Mr Brathen. "I can ring them for

56

you now, if you like?"

Mr Brathen nodded without speaking, his eyes fixed on Jingle and his forehead creased with worry.

While Fran made her call, Mr Brathen tried offering the poorly reindeer a pellet of feed from his pocket. Jingle let out a sad-sounding huff from his nostrils and turned his head away. *Poor Jingle!* Amelia thought. *He's even lost his appetite.*

It seemed like ages before Amelia heard Mrs Hope's car approaching, though it was only minutes really. Amelia and Sam opened the gate, then led Mrs Hope to the stable where Jingle had been taken.

Lying on his side now, with his eyes

57

half closed, Jingle looked sicker than ever.
Fran and Mr Brathen both looked grave
as they shuffled aside, making space for
Mrs Hope in the stall.

"Hello, Jingle," Mrs Hope said, giving
the reindeer a quick stroke. Then she
unzipped her medical bag, took out a
stethoscope and knelt to listen to Jingle's
chest. After a minute, she let out a sigh.
"I'm sorry to say Jingle has pneumonia.
We need to get him started on a course
of antibiotics straight away."

Amelia and Sam exchanged worried glances.

Mr Brathen shook his head in dismay. "But reindeer are made for snow and ice," he said. "How could he have pneumonia? And how could he have got so sick so fast?"

"Reindeer usually only contract pneumonia if they're stressed," said Mrs Hope. "Stress weakens their immune system and makes them more susceptible to illness."

"Well, with the festive season here, we have been busy," Mr Brathen said, frowning. "But only with short outings. And he's always seemed so calm."

Mrs Hope nodded kindly. "Reindeer are prey animals," she said, "which means they look fine unless they're really sick – they've adapted not to show stress. But too much noise, crowds or even getting overheated could cause them to become unwell."

"It was very noisy at the shopping centre last weekend," Sam said.

"And the children did crowd quite close," Amelia added.

Mr Brathen had turned very pale. "I didn't realise!" he said. "This is my first year keeping reindeer. I'm more used to horses. They seemed to take to everything so well. I never thought it

could make them ill!"

Mrs Hope put a hand on Mr Brathen's shoulder. "Don't worry," she said. "Once we start treating Jingle, he should recover quickly. But he'll need to be kept somewhere quiet and he won't be able to travel for a while."

"He can stay here until he's better!" Fran said. "I'll make sure he's kept quiet and comfortable."

"Thank you," Mr Brathen said. "I'd hate to put him back in the horsebox, now that I know he's sick."

"You'll need to keep an eye on Twinkle as well," Mrs Hope added. "It's possible she might become ill too. I'm

afraid it would be best if neither of them took part in the parade."

"Of course ..." Mr Brathen turned to Sam and Amelia. "I'm so sorry to let you down," he said.

Amelia did her best to hide her disappointment. "It's OK," she said. "The

most important thing is that Jingle gets well."

"We wouldn't want any animal in the parade if it made them sick," Sam added.

Once Mrs Hope

had given Jingle his jab and packed up her bag, Sam and Amelia said their goodbyes to Fran and Mr Brathen, then headed home.

"Poor Jingle," Sam said, dragging his feet a little as they walked. "And poor Mr Brathen too!"

"I know," Amelia said. "He looked so upset. And it's such a shame about the parade."

"Hmm," Sam said glumly. "I don't suppose we'll draw such a big crowd now, which means less money for the guide dog charity."

"If only the reindeer were more like Ginger and Walnut," Amelia said. "Now they've got each other, nothing seems to bother them." She suddenly stopped in her tracks. Her words had given her an idea. "Wait here!" she told Sam. Then she turned and raced back to the stables.

I have to find Fran ...

CHAPTER FIVE

On the morning of the Extravaganza, Amelia hugged herself to keep warm as she and Sam made their way through the frosty streets of Welford with Sam's parents. Even though she'd layered up beneath her elf suit, the sharp morning air still nipped at her fingers and toes.

Mac trotted at Sam's heels with his head held high and his tail wagging. He was wearing a red woolly jumper with a Christmas tree on it for warmth. Amelia glanced down at the little dog, and grinned. With his tongue lolling happily, he seemed to know just how smart he looked.

When they reached the main street, Amelia found the first few spectators had already arrived. Stallholders with steaming cups of tea and coffee put the finishing touches to their banners and

displays while Mrs Cranbourne, wearing a bright red bobble hat, hurried about checking everyone had arrived.

"We'll say goodbye now," Mr Baxter said, taking Mac's lead.

"Good luck!" Sam's mum said. "We'll be looking out for you!" Then she and Mr Baxter led Mac away to find a place to watch the parade.

People were arriving in groups now, chatting and smiling, with babies and toddlers all bundled up in snowsuits against the cold. Amelia spotted Izzy in a glittering winter fairy costume, and a few members of the choir, smartly dressed in black and white. She felt a sudden flutter

67

of nerves. *I hope everything goes to plan …*
But, a moment later, she heard the steady
clop of hooves, and smiled.

"They're here!" Sam cried, grabbing
Amelia's arm and pointing as Fran
came into view. She was dressed in an elf
costume, and leading Walnut and Ginger.

Amelia grinned. "They almost look
like reindeer!" she said, taking in the fake

antlers attached to the animals' halters, the bells around their bellies and the tinsel around their necks. Walnut pulled an old cart from the stables, painted red and decorated with more tinsel to look like a sleigh. The big horse lifted his feet smartly with each step. At his side, Ginger let out happy puffs and snorts, keeping pace with his friend.

Fran's eyes shone as Sam and Amelia hurried to greet her. "You both look great!" she said. "It was such a good idea to dress these two up," she added, gesturing to Walnut and Ginger. "They're loving it!"

"Right!" Sam said, glancing about. "Now the sleigh's here, it *must* be time to find out who Father Christmas is!" At that moment, Mrs Cranbourne bustled over carrying two heavy-looking sacks.

"Here are your sweets!" she said, handing one bag to Sam and one to Amelia. She checked her watch, then beamed with excitement. "Time for everyone to get into position!" she said.

70

"And there's our Father Christmas now!" she added, lifting a hand to wave.

Amelia turned to see a tall, stout man with a long white beard and red coat, trimmed with white, heading towards them. He wore black boots and a shiny leather belt was buckled about his huge waist. Amelia and Sam exchanged puzzled frowns.

But the big man seemed to know who they were. He grinned and waved at them. There was something familiar about him …

"In you get, then!" said Mrs Cranbourne, putting a hand on Amelia's back to guide her forwards. Fran was standing at the front of the cart, holding Walnut's reins.

Amelia stepped in, feeling a thrill of excitement as the cart shifted slightly with her weight. It moved even more as

the tall man playing Santa climbed in beside her, taking up most of the little bench so that Amelia had to shuffle right over. Last of all, Sam squeezed in on Santa's other side.

"Are we all ready, then?" Mrs Cranbourne asked.

"I certainly am," said Santa, then he held his round belly with both hands, leaned back and let out a booming "*Ho, ho, ho!*".

Suddenly, with a jolt of surprise, Amelia recognised the man's gravelly voice. "Mr Ferguson!" she cried. "Is that you?"

CHAPTER SIX

Mr Ferguson pulled the long, white beard away from his mouth, giving Amelia a glimpse of his own stubbly beard underneath.

"I've got a lot of extra padding," he said, patting his big, round belly, "but it's me all right!"

Amelia gaped in astonishment. "But I thought you weren't even coming!" she said.

"You just pretended to be grumpy about the parade to trick us!" Sam said.

Mr Ferguson shrugged his shoulders. "Mrs Cranbourne twisted my arm. It's all a load of nonsense." He sounded gruff, but Amelia could see from the sparkle in his eyes that he was really enjoying himself.

"I told you that you'd never guess!"

Mrs Cranbourne said. "Now, I'm just going to make sure everyone's in their places. It's not long until we start, and there's already quite a crowd!"

Glancing about, Amelia was surprised to see how quickly the street had filled up. Smiling faces lined both sides of the road, and the cake stall and tombola were already surrounded by customers. The air was filled with cheerful voices.

"Everyone from Welford must be here!" Amelia said.

"And Walton too, I reckon," Mr Ferguson added.

Looking back, Amelia spotted Izzy and Caleb on either side of the choir, each holding a donation bucket. She caught Izzy's eye and waved. In front of her school friends, Amelia could see the nursery children holding hands in pairs, red-cheeked and shiny-eyed from the cold. They all wore costumes from the nativity under their coats. A little girl dressed as an angel with a tinsel halo was at the front of the group, beside a boy with a gold cardboard crown. Both

had such solemn expressions that Amelia
had to bite her lip to contain her grin.
Oh, they look so adorable!

The choir's portable sound system gave
a crackle, and then the opening chords of
Jingle Bells rang out loudly. Fran clicked
her tongue and Walnut and Ginger
started walking. Amelia's tummy gave a
skip as the cart lurched into motion.

"Ho ho ho!" boomed Mr Ferguson.
"Merry Christmas!" And with that, the
parade was off.

Here we go! Amelia thought. Her cheeks
soon ached from grinning as she and
Sam tossed handfuls of sweets into the
crowd. They passed houses and shops

strung with Christmas lights. Most of the
trees glinted with lights too, and tinsel
decorated the streetlamps. The choir's
singing rang out above the cheers of the
crowd and mingled with Mr Ferguson's
merry chuckle and the clip-clop of
Walnut and Ginger's hooves.

As they turned a corner, Amelia
spotted Paloma smiling and waving
with her parents. Mr Ferguson waved

back at them, grinning at his niece and
giving her a wink. The little girl tugged
her mum's hand, jumping up and down.
Amelia grinned. *If only Paloma knew it was
her uncle! She'd never believe it* … Amelia
tossed a huge handful of sweets towards
the little girl, who kept waving until they
were out of sight.

A little further along the road, they
passed a trestle table covered in leaflets.

Amelia's mum and gran both stood beside it, holding buckets. A tall man wearing dark glasses stood with them, holding the harness of his glossy-coated Golden Retriever. The guide dog sat smartly at his owner's feet, his eyes alert.

Amelia's mum smiled and gave her a big thumbs-up, then pointed into her bucket. "We've already raised loads of money!" she called. Amelia grinned back.

Sitting behind Walnut and Ginger, with *Deck the Halls* ringing out loudly behind her and the streets lined with waving, smiling people, Amelia felt so happy she wanted to cheer. And despite the frosty chill in the air, she felt warm and toasty inside. *The parade is a huge success!*

By the time Sam and Amelia had finished helping with the clear-up operation and changed out of their costumes, the streetlamps had come on and frost glittered on the roads and pavements. The fairy lights in the trees shone brightly in the dusk as Sam and

Amelia made their way to the stables to check on Jingle.

They found Mrs Hope's car already parked on the drive, and as they reached Jingle's stable, they could hear the vet inside, speaking with Mr Brathen.

"I hope Jingle's all right!" Amelia said, feeling a stab of fear for the reindeer as they hurried into the stable. But she didn't have to worry for long. As soon as she saw Mr Brathen's smile, she breathed a sigh of relief. Jingle was standing up in his stable now, his eyes bright and clear.

"He's doing really well," Mrs Hope said.

"And Twinkle hasn't shown any signs

of getting sick," Mr Brathen added. "What a relief! I shan't be doing any more Christmas engagements with the reindeer from now on. I'd much rather they were happy and healthy!"

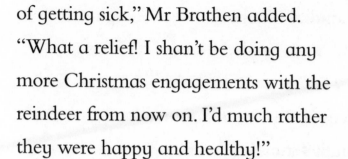

He turned to Sam and gave him a wink. "Now, young man, I've heard your parents make the best breakfast in town, so I'll be staying at your B&B until Jingle's fully recovered. How would you two like to feed him a special treat, now he's got his appetite back?"

"Yes, please!" Sam and Amelia said together.

"Come on then," Mr Brathen said. He reached into his pocket and drew out a handful of what looked like spinach.

Sam wrinkled his nose. "This is a treat?" he said doubtfully, taking a few leaves. But when Sam reached over the stable door, Jingle lifted his head, eyeing the greens with interest. As Sam held the greens under Jingle's nose, the reindeer put out a long pink tongue and scooped

them into his mouth.

"That's right," Mr Brathen said. "Reindeer love their vegetables."

"Leafy greens and mushrooms

are actually their favourite foods," Mrs Hope added.

"Wow," Sam said, as Jingle chomped away happily. "In that case, they can have all my Christmas sprouts!"

"And mine," Amelia said.

As the four of them laughed, their breath rising into the cold evening air, Amelia felt a warm rush of contentment spread through her whole body. And then another thought struck her – one that made her heart leap. *There's only one more week until Christmas!*

STORY TWO:
Reindeer Rescue

CHAPTER ONE

On the morning of Christmas Eve, Amelia stirred groggily. Something was pricking her face. She felt it again and realised what it was – a little paw with tiny claws. She opened her eyes a crack to see Star's pink nose almost pressed against her own.

 As Amelia
blinked and woke
up properly, Star
purred loudly and
nuzzled Amelia's
cheek with a chilly nose.

"Hello," Amelia said, stroking her
little cat. Then she sat up and looked
about. The house felt somehow different.
Quieter than usual … with a sort of
muffled feeling. And even with the
curtains closed, a pearly brightness filled
the room. *No way!*

Amelia set Star on the floor, leapt out
of bed and crossed to the window. She
threw the curtains open, and gasped.

Every twig, every leaf, every fence
post was covered in a thick, puffy layer
of snow. Not even the tips of the grass
showed on the lawn, and her gran's
flowerbeds were just lumps in the pristine
whiteness. Amelia remembered with a
sudden jolt of excitement that Mrs Hope
would be picking her up soon, so they
could check on Mr Brathen's reindeer.

I hope she can get through all this snow!

Amelia dressed quickly and hurried downstairs to find her mum and her gran at the kitchen table, drinking coffee and listening to the radio.

"Have you ever seen so much snow?" Amelia's mum asked.

"I know!" Amelia said. "It's so deep. I can't wait to get out in it!" She poured herself some cereal and took a seat beside her gran.

As Amelia munched her breakfast, she racked her brains, trying to think of what she might get Sam for Christmas when she went shopping with her mum that afternoon. *Nothing like leaving things to the*

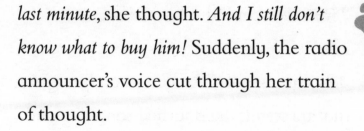

last minute, she thought. *And I still don't know what to buy him!* Suddenly, the radio announcer's voice cut through her train of thought.

"Well, I hope you've all finished your Christmas shopping!" the man's voice said cheerfully. "*All main roads in and out of York are currently blocked, and with more snow in the forecast, they're unlikely to reopen until after the festive period ...*"

"Oh no!" Amelia set down her spoon and looked at her mum in alarm. "That means we can't go shopping later like we planned. And I still don't have anything to give Sam!"

"Don't worry," Amelia's gran said.

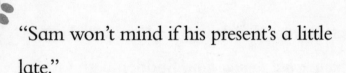

"Sam won't mind if his present's a little late."

"I suppose not," Amelia said glumly. At that moment, the doorbell rang. "That will be Mrs Hope!" she said, doing her best to push her disappointment aside. She kissed her mum and Gran goodbye and grabbed her coat and hat.

"Ready to go?" Mrs Hope asked as Amelia answered the door. Sam smiled and waved from the back seat of the Hopes' car.

"I was worried you might not make it with all this snow," Amelia said to Mrs Hope, as she climbed in beside Sam.

"Luckily I've got winter tyres," Mrs

Hope said, fastening her seat belt. "But if it snows any more, it will be too dangerous to drive at all."

They barely passed any other cars on the short drive to the stables, but plenty of people were out and about, shovelling snow, or throwing gritting salt on their drives to melt the ice.

As Mrs Hope's car drew close to the stables, Sam pointed out of the window towards the paddock. "There they are!" he said.

Amelia spotted both reindeer, racing up and down the field together. "They look like they're having fun!" she said.

"I expect they are," Mrs Hope said,

parking the car. "Reindeer are one of the few animals that aren't bothered by snow."

They all got out of the car and the children ran over to the fence. Amelia felt a rush of happiness as she watched the two reindeer playing, while all around them the white countryside glittered in the morning sun. She grinned at Sam. "It looks just like a scene from a Christmas film!"

CHAPTER TWO

Sam, Amelia and Mrs Hope found Mr
Brathen leaning on the paddock fence
watching Twinkle and Jingle play.

"Hello there," he said, smiling. "Those
antibiotics seem to have done the trick.
Jingle's back to his old self. And he's
making the most of the weather, too!"

"He certainly looks healthy," Mrs Hope said. "If you can coax him over, I'll give him a check-up."

Mr Brathen fished in his pocket and pulled out a few wrinkled-looking mushrooms. "Come, Jingle! Come, Twinkle!" he called. The two reindeer lifted their heads and wheeled round, veering towards him. Mr Brathen handed Sam and Amelia a couple of mushrooms each.

"You can give those to Twinkle," he said. Then he opened the paddock gate for Mrs Hope and followed her inside.

While Mrs Hope examined Jingle in the field with Mr Brathen, Sam and

102

Amelia held
their hands
out over the
top of the
fence.

"Come,
Twinkle!" Sam
called. The

caramel-coloured reindeer slowly made
her way towards him, eyeing the treats in
his hand.

Amelia noticed something interesting
about the reindeer's feet. They hardly
seemed to leave tracks in the snow at all.
"See how flat and spread out her hooves
are!" she said to Sam, her voice hushed so

as not to scare the reindeer. "I guess it's so she can walk on top of the snow."

"Yes, like she's wearing snowshoes," Sam whispered. Then he fell silent, hardly breathing, as Twinkle sidled right up to the fence and sniffed at the mushroom in his hand. The reindeer picked up the food with her soft, flexible lips and started chewing, while Sam stood very still, smiling.

Amelia took off her glove and slowly put

out a hand to scratch the fur on Twinkle's head. The reindeer closed her eyes in pleasure, and Amelia marvelled at how thick Twinkle's coat felt. *No wonder it keeps her so warm!*

After Twinkle had eaten the last of the mushrooms from Sam and Amelia's hands, she trotted off to join Jingle. Mrs Hope and Brathen came back through the gate, both smiling broadly.

"Jingle's made a full recovery!" Mrs Hope said.

"Which means I can take them home again," Mr Brathen said, "as soon as the snow clears. In the meantime, I think we should make the most of it." He looked at Sam and Amelia with a playful glint in his eyes. "How about we hitch the reindeer up for a sleigh ride?" he asked.

"Yes, please!" Amelia and Sam said together.

Mrs Hope winced apologetically. "I'm afraid I have to get back to Animal Ark. Julia's on reception, and I need to take her home before more snow comes and we're all stuck inside for good."

Amelia felt a rush of disappointment. It must have showed on her face, because Mr Brathen smiled. "Well, if you can spare these two, I can drop them back home in the sleigh?" he said. "That is, if it's all right with their parents."

"Here," Mrs Hope said to Amelia and Sam. "You can borrow my phone to call them."

After Sam and Amelia had spoken to their parents and said goodbye to Mrs Hope, Mr Brathen called his reindeer over and clipped their lead ropes to their halters. Amelia felt a flutter of nerves as Mr Brathen handed her Jingle's rope. But as she started walking, she found that, while she slipped and skidded a little on the churned-up snow, the

surefooted reindeer followed with no
problems at all.

When they reached the stable
courtyard, Mr Brathen showed Sam and
Amelia how to clip the reindeer's leads
to tie rings in the wall near the waiting
sleigh.

"Now, just like horses, don't approach
reindeer from behind because they might
kick," Mr Brathen said. "But unlike
horses, you've always got to keep an eye
on their antlers, too. They're quite sharp
at this time of year. I'll harness Jingle
first. Watch carefully, and I'll let you two
harness Twinkle."

After fetching two bell-covered

harnesses, Mr Brathen showed Sam and
Amelia how to fasten the padded collar
around Jingle's neck and buckle it at the
side. Next, he buckled another thick strap,
called the girth, around the reindeer's
middle. Finally, he clipped a D-ring near
the back of the harness to a long pole
attached to the sleigh.

"Your turn now," said Mr Brathen

when he was finished.

Amelia approached Twinkle slowly, hardly daring to breathe as she picked up the second harness. But the reindeer stood perfectly still, waiting patiently while she and Sam buckled her collar. Between them, with a lot of ducking to avoid Twinkle's pointy antlers, they soon finished harnessing the reindeer and attached her to the sleigh.

"Good job!" Mr Brathen said, after inspecting their work. He connected a short tie rope between the reindeer, unclipped them from their tethers and attached reins to their halters. "In you get!" he told Sam and Amelia. "We are

110

all ready to go!"

Mr Brathen sat in the front of the
sleigh and took hold of the reindeer's
reins. Amelia clambered in behind him
with Sam, squeezing her hands together
excitedly.

"There are only a few commands you
need to know," Mr Brathen told them.
"*Mush* means go, *haw* means left and *gee*
means right. Oh, and *whoa* for stop, of
course."

Amelia whispered the commands to
herself, trying to memorise them.

"Mush!" Mr Brathen said, then clicked
his tongue. The reindeer leaped into
motion, tugging the sleigh forwards and

leaving Amelia's tummy behind.

"Woo hoo!" Sam cried.

Amelia leaned forward excitedly, her breath catching in her throat as they flew over the snowy courtyard, bells jingling and the cold wind whipping their faces.

"Haw!" Mr Brathen called, and the reindeer made a sweeping turn to the left, carrying them neatly through the courtyard gate and out on to the snow-

covered track leading up to the fields.

Amelia hung on to the bench as the reindeer sped onwards, pulling the sleigh behind them as if it weighed nothing at all. They obeyed each command from Mr Brathen in perfect time with each other.

"It looks like the reindeer are enjoying it," Amelia said, noticing their quick, light steps and the eager way they stretched

their shaggy necks forwards.

"They love it!" Mr Brathen said.
"They're never happier than when
they're pulling the sleigh. Whoa!" he
called, and the reindeer began to slow.
Once the sleigh had stopped, Mr Brathen
turned to Sam and Amelia.

"Now, how would you two like to have
a go driving?" he asked.

Amelia could hardly believe what she'd
heard. "Yes, please!" she said.

"That would be amazing!" Sam said.

"So, who's going first?" Mr Brathen
asked.

"You can if you like," Amelia told Sam,
who swapped places with Mr Brathen.

Sam took the reins in his hands, then turned to face them with an anxious smile.

"You can do it!" Mr Brathen said.

Sam squared his shoulders, then clicked his tongue. "Mush!" he called. The reindeer shot forwards and Sam let out a whoop of delight.

After Sam had taken them for a drive all the way around the field, it was Amelia's turn to drive. She held tight to the reins as they sped over the snow.

"Gee! Gee!" she cried, as the reindeer approached a hedgerow. They cornered in a sweeping arc, carrying the sleigh past the hedge, then back out into the open field. Amelia's teeth soon throbbed with cold from grinning into the freezing wind, but she was having so much fun she didn't care. *Driving reindeer is the best thing ever!*

CHAPTER THREE

"That was amazing!" Amelia said, as she
and Sam walked the final stretch back
to his house. Mr Brathen had dropped
them nearby. He was still staying at
the B&B himself, but he needed to take
the reindeer back to the stables. "I can't
believe Mr Brathen said we're naturals."

"We'll definitely have to do it again!"
Sam said. "After all, he's going to be
stuck here a while."

"It was nice of Fran's parents to say he
could spend Christmas with them," said
Amelia.

As they approached a turn in the road,
Amelia heard the growl of an engine
starting up. Almost at once, it chugged to
a stop.

"Sounds like someone's having trouble
with their car," Sam said. "Maybe we
can help."

But, when they rounded the corner,
instead of a car they found Mr Ferguson
and his motorbike. The engine roared

again, then died.
Mr Ferguson
climbed off,
huffing out
a sigh of
frustration
as Sam and
Amelia reached him.

"Are you stuck?" Sam asked.

"You could say that," Mr Ferguson
replied, crossly. "I'm supposed to be well
on the way to Walton by now, to visit
my sister for Christmas, but I'll never
make it through all this snow! The bike's
too heavy to push." He scowled down
at the machine. "I'll just have to carry

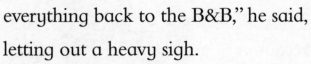

everything back to the B&B," he said, letting out a heavy sigh.

"We'll help!" Sam said. "We're heading there anyway."

"Thank you," Mr Ferguson said, managing a smile. "I'll be glad of a hand. It'll take more than one trip by myself." He unstrapped a big box from the back of his bike, then a holdall and his laptop bag.

"If you two can manage the box between you, I'll take the bags," he said. "But be careful with it."

"What's in it?" Amelia asked.

"You can take a look if you like," Mr Ferguson said, his voice sounding glum.

Amelia
opened
the box and
gasped with
surprise. Inside, she
could see the pointed
rooftop of a wooden
dolls' house, complete
with painted tiles and two chimneys. She
closed the lid again.

"Do think Paloma will like it?" Mr
Ferguson asked.

"Are you kidding?" Amelia said. "Of
course she will! Where did you get it?"

Mr Ferguson looked down bashfully.

"You made it yourself, didn't you?"

Sam said. "That's why you didn't want to buy the dolls' house in the toyshop!"

Mr Ferguson shrugged. "I was really looking forward to surprising Paloma," he said. "But I guess that will have to wait until after Christmas now." Picking up their parcels, they all started off together through the snow.

When Sam, Amelia and Mr Ferguson reached the Bed and Breakfast, Sam's mum threw the door open before they could ring the doorbell.

"Come inside quickly!" she said. "You must be frozen." Sam and Amelia set the big box down in the hall, then took off their boots and coats.

"I had a feeling you might be back," Mrs Baxter told Mr Ferguson, smiling sympathetically at his grumpy expression. "I cooked extra stew, just in case. And you'll have to spend Christmas with us. Not as a guest, of course, but as family."

Mr Ferguson's eyes opened wide. "Really?" he said. "That's very kind of you." He nodded slowly as if thinking, then gave a final decisive nod. "Yes, thank you, Mrs B. I'm really touched by your offer." But despite what Mr Ferguson said, Amelia still thought he looked disappointed.

"Paloma will be just as pleased to get

123

her present after Christmas," she said.

"Ooh! Speaking of presents …" Sam said, ducking towards the staircase. "Don't come upstairs yet, Amelia. I still need to wrap yours."

Amelia felt a horrible sinking feeling. *I still don't have anything for Sam!* she thought. *I have to think of something. And soon!*

"Come through to the dining room," Mrs Baxter told Amelia and Mr Ferguson. "Lunch is almost ready. Sam – don't take too long."

Sitting down at the Baxters' dining table, with a huge plate of steaming vegetable stew before her, Amelia

suddenly realised how hungry she was.
Sam soon joined them, and just as they'd
all started eating, they heard the front
door bang. A moment later, Mr Baxter
came into the dining room.

125

"It's started snowing again!" he said merrily. "It's like a blizzard out there. The village is pretty much snowed in now, and the shops have all shut. I hope you've saved some stew for me. I'm starving!"

As Mr Baxter sat down at the table and helped himself to a big plate of stew, Amelia found her own appetite suddenly gone. *Oh no! Now I can't even get Sam a present from the local shops*, she thought. *He's going to think I didn't even care enough to try!*

CHAPTER FOUR

Dragging Sam's plastic sledge behind them, and with Mac bounding ahead, sniffing and snuffling at the snow, it took Sam and Amelia half an hour to reach the hill near the stables. The snow had stopped while they had eaten their lunch, but the clouds still looked heavy. As they arrived, Amelia could hear screams and shouts from other children sledging down the hill.

Sam unclipped Mac from his lead, and they both watched him tear off up the slope, skittering from side to side as if chasing imaginary prey, his tail sticking up and his tongue flapping. Sam and Amelia followed Mac up the hill more slowly, pulling the sledge. When they reached the top, they found a clear run of snow and took their seats with Sam in front and Amelia behind.

"Tuck in your feet!" Sam cried, then he and Amelia pushed off.

"Wheeee!" they shouted as they

plunged down the steep slope, the wind
in their faces.

"Ruff, ruff!" they heard from behind
them. As they started to slow, Amelia
glanced back to see Mac careening
down the hill after them. And, as the
sledge slowed, she realised Mac wasn't
going to stop …

THUMP! Mac bowled
into the back of her,
tumbled over in the
snow, then leapt
up to lick first
her face,
then

Sam's, his eyes shining and his tail wagging frantically.

"Bleurgh!" Amelia said, grinning as she wiped her face.

"All right, Mac," Sam said, pushing his little dog away. "You can come on the sledge with us next time."

When they got back up the slope, they climbed into the sledge again and Sam tucked Mac between his feet. As Amelia pushed off at the top of the hill, Mac let

out a yip of excitement. He barked and barked the whole way down. Near the bottom, Amelia felt a jolt as the sledge hit a rough patch in the snow. Her stomach lurched as the sledge tipped forwards and she flew through the air. *WHUMP!*

Amelia landed in a tangled heap with Sam and Mac. The Westie scrambled up and raced away, too excited to wait, while Sam and Amelia brushed themselves off and climbed the hill once more.

After another few runs, the grey light had started to fade and snow began to fall again. Looking about, Amelia noticed they were the last people left on the slope. "We should head back," she said. "We don't want to get caught out in the dark."

"Agreed," Sam said. "I think my toes have actually started to freeze!" He cupped his hands to his mouth. "Here, Mac!" he shouted.

Amelia peered into the shadowy greyness but couldn't see anything moving.

"Here, Mac!" Sam called again. This time, Amelia spotted a small white furball

 barrelling over the snow, mist rising with his warm breath.

"Phew!" Amelia said. "I'm glad he came. Looking for a white dog in all this snow wouldn't be easy!"

As they started back along the darkening road, the only sound they could hear was the crunch of their footsteps and the whisper of the sledge they were dragging behind them.

Before they had gone far, Mac started to lag behind.

"Are you tired, Mac?" Sam said, turning. "You can ride in the sledge—Mac!" he said again, his tone suddenly urgent. "What's wrong?"

Amelia looked at the Westie and saw that his whole body was shaking.

"Maybe he's cold?" she said. But then Mac stumbled, his legs going out from under him. He lay in the snow, looking dazed and shivering violently. Amelia felt a jolt of fear. *There's something wrong with him!*

"Mac!" Sam cried, kneeling beside his dog. Amelia could hear the panic in her friend's voice. Her own throat felt tight with worry as she watched Sam cradle

the little dog in his arms. Mac blinked up at Sam with a sad, confused look in his eyes. He was shaking so much

his teeth started to chatter.

"What should we do?" Sam asked. "I think he's really sick!"

Amelia took a deep breath, trying to stay calm despite the churning feeling in her tummy. "We need to get him to Animal Ark, urgently." She thought about knocking on someone's door to ask for a lift or to borrow a phone to call her mother, but then she remembered no cars could drive in the thick snow. *And Animal Ark's over half an hour's walk away!*

Amelia looked down at the trembling puppy to see his tongue hanging out, drool dripping from his jaws. *He might*

135

not make it that long! We need another way
to get to Animal Ark. Amelia's eyes fell
on Sam's sledge, and she had an idea.
Of course!

"Wait here," she told Sam. "Keep Mac
as warm as you can. I'm going to the
stables to ask Mr Brathen to take us in
his sleigh!"

"Please hurry!" Sam said, his eyes wide
with worry.

Amelia broke into a run, her boots
sinking deep into the snow with each
step and her heart thundering in her
chest. By the time she reached the stables
she was breathless and sweating all over.
She found the courtyard deserted, but a

light shone through the
reception window. Amelia
hurried inside.

"Fran?" she called. "Mr
Brathen?" But there was
no answer.

What do I do now? Amelia thought. *I
can't just take the reindeer without asking!*
Then she spotted a card for Mr Brathen's
business pinned to the noticeboard beside
the telephone. She picked up the receiver
and called the number on the card.

"Hello?" Mr Brathen answered.

"Hello, it's Amelia Haywood. I really
need your help. Sam's dog Mac has fallen
very ill, right by the stables, and we need

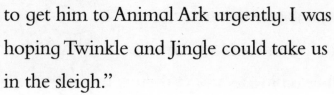

to get him to Animal Ark urgently. I was hoping Twinkle and Jingle could take us in the sleigh."

"Oh! Poor Mac!" Mr Brathen said. "I wish I could help, but I'm at the B&B now. It'll take me a while to get back to the stables."

Amelia had an idea, but she bit her lip, hardly daring to ask. *What if he says no* ... But then she blurted the question out. "How about I harness the reindeer and take them?" she said. "I'm sure I remember how, and I'll bring them straight back. Mac's very sick." There was a long pause at the other end of the line. Amelia could almost hear Mr Brathen

thinking. *Please, please say yes!*

"All right," Mr Brathen said at last. "It
sounds like an emergency. I know you're

responsible, and Jingle and Twinkle will

do as you say. But be careful! I'll give

your parents a call and let them know

where you and Sam are, then I'll meet

you at the surgery."

"Thank you!" Amelia cried. She put

down the receiver and swallowed hard.

Now for the tricky part!

CHAPTER FIVE

Amelia hurried back to the courtyard and pulled the cover off the reindeer's sleigh. Forcing herself to breathe steadily, so as not to spook the animals, she opened Twinkle and Jingle's stall. The reindeer lifted their heads and let out snorts, as if they were pleased to see her.

Amelia took off her gloves. Trying to ignore the butterflies in her stomach, she gave each reindeer a quick stroke, then attached ropes to their halters. *I can do this!*

"We're going for a ride," Amelia told the two reindeer, keeping her voice as calm as she could as she led them out into the snowy courtyard. She clipped

the reindeer's leads to the tie rings near the sleigh. To her relief, Twinkle and Jingle stood still as she slipped on their harnesses. At first, Amelia fumbled at the buckles, her cold, numb fingers shaking as adrenaline rushed through her. But she forced herself to slow down, and somehow managed to fasten the buckles and clip the harnesses to the sleigh. Then, taking both reindeer's leads in her hands, Amelia climbed into the sleigh. *Here goes!* she thought.

Amelia took a steadying breath of freezing air, then called, "Mush!" Both reindeer started off together, trotting neatly over the snow. Amelia's tummy flipped as the sleigh rushed forwards.

With their harness bells ringing, Twinkle and Jingle quickly picked up

speed, letting out happy snorts. As the
sleigh's runners swished cleanly over the
deep snow, Amelia gave the reins a tug.
"Gee!" she called. The reindeer cornered
neatly. Amelia leaned into the turn as the
sleigh sailed around the bend. Soon, she
could see the shadowy forms of Sam and
Mac ahead.

"Whoa!" she called and the reindeer
slowed to a stop. Amelia leapt down from
her seat and raced towards Sam.

"How is he?" Amelia asked. But even
before Sam could answer, Amelia knew
Mac was much worse. The poor Westie
was panting heavily. Sam had wrapped
him in his scarf, and Amelia could see a

patch of sick on the fabric.

"He's really ill!" Sam said, his voice cracking with emotion. "Let's go, now!"

Sam carried the Westie to the sleigh and clambered into the back seat, holding Mac on his lap. Her heart racing, Amelia took the reins once more.

"Mush!" she called. And they were off! Street lamps and houses decked with Christmas lights whizzed past in a blur as Amelia drove the sleigh over the smooth, deep snow. Each time she called a command, the reindeer obeyed at once, their bells jingling and their quick feet hardly seeming to touch the snowy ground. Amelia had forgotten to put her gloves back on, and her fingers felt numb on the reins, but it didn't matter. She glanced back to see Sam bent low over Mac, cradling his little dog tightly. *Please hang on, Mac!* Amelia pleaded silently.

She leaned forward, every fibre of her being urging the reindeer to run faster through the dusky streets. Her pulse beat loudly in her ears as they sped over the untouched snow.

When Amelia finally brought the sleigh to a halt in front of Animal Ark, her heart was hammering so hard it felt like it might burst. She leaped down from her seat, quickly clipped the reindeer's tie ropes back on and attached them to a lamppost. By the time she had finished securing Twinkle and Jingle, Sam was already inside with Mac. Amelia hurried after him.

Mrs Hope was sitting at the reception desk. "Mac's in with Mr Hope," she said quickly. "You can go right through – I'll keep an eye on the reindeer."

Amelia found poor Mac hunched on the assessment table, panting and shivering, while Mr Hope felt him all over with gloved hands. Though Amelia had been in the room countless times helping with other animals, it hadn't prepared her for how awful it felt seeing Mac there. His white muzzle was stained with sick as he hung his head, his ears and tail drooping. Sam looked on, still wearing his coat, his face grey with worry.

"From what you've told me, I think Mac must have eaten some gritting salt," Mr Hope said at last. "We've had another puppy and two cats in with the same thing today. Gritting salt can make animals very sick."

"He must have eaten some while we were sledging," Sam said in a small voice. "Or maybe on the walk through the village. He keeps on eating things he shouldn't! I was afraid it would make him sick, and I was right …"

"Don't worry," Mr Hope said. "He'll have to stay in overnight on a drip. But now we're treating him, he should make a full recovery."

Amelia suddenly realised that she'd been holding her breath, and let it all out at once.

Sam blinked back tears. "So … he's going to be OK?" he said.

Mr Hope nodded, smiling kindly. "You did the right thing getting him here so quickly. I'm going to take him out to the back now, and get his treatment started right away. It's probably better if you stay here."

"Goodbye, Mac," Sam said, leaning right down so his face almost touched the little dog's. Mac gave Sam's nose a lick, then Mr Hope scooped him gently into his arms. "You'll feel better soon," Sam called after his Westie.

Sam and Amelia went back into the waiting room to find Mr Brathen had arrived, red-faced from hurrying through the snow.

"How's Mac?" he asked at once.

Amelia wanted to run over and hug him. "He's going to be OK, thanks to you!" she said. "He ate some gritting salt and it made him really sick."

"Thank you so much for letting us borrow your reindeer," Sam said to Mr Brathen. Then he turned to Amelia. "And thank you, too. I think you saved Mac's life!"

"I'm so relieved to hear Mac's going to be all right," Mr Brathen said. "I wouldn't normally let anyone drive my reindeer without me, but I definitely made the right decision. I've checked Jingle and Twinkle over, Amelia, and you harnessed them perfectly."

"They were brilliant!" Amelia said. "They stood really still while I hitched them up, and obeyed all my commands. I'm going to save them a double helping of sprouts!"

"It was certainly a good thing the reindeer were close by when Mac fell ill," Mrs Hope said, from her seat at the reception desk. "It made all the difference getting him here as quickly as you did, and there's no other way to travel at the moment."

Looking through the window, Amelia could see downy flakes of snow falling in the halos of light surrounding the streetlamps. And, now that her worry

for Mac had passed, she was struck
with a sudden idea that sent a tingle of
excitement through her. She turned to
Mr Brathen.

"I know someone else who could
do with a ride," she said. "If Jingle and
Twinkle aren't too tired, do you think we
could make one more trip?"

Squished in the back of the sleigh with
dark, snowy fields speeding past on either
side and bells ringing in her ears, Amelia
grinned into the icy wind. Mr Ferguson
sat between Amelia and Sam, clutching
his bags and the box containing his

homemade dolls' house. Mr Brathen had the reins. Ahead, Twinkle and Jingle flew over the snow.

Before long, Amelia spotted the glittering lights of a town in the darkness ahead. The sleigh swished down the deserted roads and before long, Mr Brathen pulled the reindeer to a halt beside a small, pretty cottage on the outskirts of Walton.

Sam and Amelia climbed out and waited by the sleigh as Mr Ferguson knocked on the door.

Yellow light spilled out on to the snow as Mr Ferguson's sister opened the door with Paloma at her side. Paloma's eyes opened wide and she let out a shriek

 of delight as she spotted her uncle.

Mr Ferguson wrapped the little girl in a hug, his eyes closing tight as he squeezed his niece. Sam and Amelia

exchanged wide grins at the sight of them both so happy.

Thanks to Twinkle and Jingle, Mr Ferguson will get to spend Christmas with his family after all! Amelia thought.

CHAPTER SIX

Back at home by the fire, curled up with her knitting, Amelia told her mum and Gran all about her day.

"I'm so glad we could help Mr Ferguson get to his family for Christmas," she said.

"It sounds like everything worked

out," Amelia's mum said. "I'm glad Mr Brathen told me what was going on. I was getting ready to send out a search party! And although I wouldn't normally approve of you sleigh-riding by yourself, I think you did the right thing. I'm very proud of you."

Amelia let out a small sigh. "I still feel bad for Sam, though. He's going to miss having Mac at home for Christmas. And on top of that, I didn't even manage to find him a present. There's no way to get one now."

From her rocking chair, Amelia's gran let out a giggle. "The answer's right under your nose, silly!" she said.

160

Amelia frowned for a moment, puzzled,
then looked down at the knitting in
her lap. It was supposed to be a warm
blanket for the animals at Animal Ark,
but it hadn't turned out quite as she'd
hoped. It was far too long and narrow.

"Of course!" she said.

When Amelia woke on Christmas
morning, it was still almost dark outside
but she could just about see exciting

bulges in the stocking at the foot of
her bed. With a flutter in her tummy,
she hurriedly tugged the stocking on
to her lap. Star, lying curled at her side,
stretched and yawned, then watched
with interest as Amelia pulled out each
item – chocolate coins, a candy cane,
an adorable puppy cuddly toy and an
orange. There was even an
iced biscuit in the shape of
a snowman.
Yum!
"Come on,
Star," Amelia
said, jumping
out of bed.

"I've got a present for you downstairs!"

Amelia found her mum and Gran in the kitchen making breakfast. Christmas carols were playing softly on the radio.

"Merry Christmas!" Amelia said.

"Merry Christmas!" her mum and her gran both said together, smiling happily.

After a breakfast of scrambled eggs, Amelia, her mum and her gran exchanged presents. Last of all, Amelia helped Star unwrap her new toy mouse. The little cat's eyes followed Amelia's every movement as she removed the shiny paper. Amelia dangled the mouse by the tail before her cat, but Star's eyes were still fixed on the ball of discarded

 paper. She wiggled her bottom, then pounced. Amelia giggled. "If you like wrapping paper, I guess we have enough fun here to last you until next Christmas," she said, looking at all the scraps strewn about on the floor.

The telephone started to ring in the hall and Amelia's mum went to answer it. "It's your dad, Amelia," she called. After saying "Merry Christmas", Amelia's mum handed the receiver to her.

"Hello, love! Happy Christmas!"

Amelia's dad said. For a moment, Amelia eyes prickled and her throat tightened at the sound of his voice – it was the first Christmas they had spent apart. But, as her dad started to chat about the firework display he planned to take her to on New Year's Eve, and the dinner they'd cook together, she started to feel cheerful again. *I'm lucky, really*, she thought as she put down the phone. *My mum and my dad are both happy, and I get to have fun with both of them.*

After helping her mum tidy away the breakfast things, Amelia pulled on her boots and coat and, taking her wrapped present with her, headed out into the snow. The sun had risen fully now, glinting through chinks in the clouds, making the snow shine so brightly it was dazzling. Most people had cleared the pavements in front of their houses, which made walking easier than it had been yesterday. She soon reached the door to

the B&B. After she knocked, she heard feet thundering down the stairs inside.

"Merry Christmas!" Sam said, grinning as he flung open the

door. For a moment, Amelia stood on the doorstep, feeling as if something was missing. She realised what it was with a pang – normally Mac would have come rushing out to greet her.

Amelia followed Sam into the warmth of the living room and handed him his present. She held her breath as he unwrapped the paper. *I really hope he likes it!*

Sam carefully pulled out the length of knitted fabric inside, running a hand over the soft, red wool. "A scarf!" he said, grinning. "Just what I needed!"

"I made it myself," Amelia said. "It can replace the one Mac was sick on."

"It must have taken you ages!" Sam said, looping the scarf round his neck. "I love it. Thank you!" Sam handed her a flat, square package in return.

Amelia opened it and found a framed picture of her and Sam sitting in the sleigh pulled by Ginger and Walnut, with Mr Ferguson as Father Christmas between them. Sam grinned at her look of surprise.

"My dad took it when we were in the parade," he said.

"It's perfect!"
Amelia said.

Amelia and Sam had one last visit to make before Christmas lunch. Although Animal Ark wasn't officially open, the Hopes had told them they could pop by any time.

As Mr Hope opened the door wearing an apron, a rush of warmth enveloped Amelia, along with the smell of roasting turkey and a blast of Christmas music.

"Come in!" Mr Hope said. "I'll just get Emily."

Sam and Amelia hurried into the

reception area, and a few moments later the Hopes reappeared. Mrs Hope was wearing a paper hat and finishing off a mince pie.

"Merry Christmas!" she said.

Amelia handed Mr Hope the wrapped box of ginger biscuits. "It's from both of us," she told him as he opened it.

"Thank you – these are our favourites!" Mr Hope said. "Now we've got a surprise for you, too."

Mr and Mrs Hope led Sam and Amelia through to Animal Ark's "hotel", where sick pets stayed overnight. As soon as they went through the door, Amelia heard an excited yip. *Mac!*

The little white dog started racing around his cage in tight circles as soon as he spotted them, then he jumped up at the bars, whimpering with excitement.

"He looks so much better!" Sam said, putting his hands through the bars for Mac to lick.

"He's doing great," Mr Hope said. "And since you managed to get him to us so quickly, he's recovering nicely. In fact, he's ready to go home!"

"That's brilliant news!" Sam said. Mr Hope opened

the door to the cage, and Mac leapt out into Sam's arms. He started licking his owner's face all over, while Sam grinned and wrinkled his nose.

Back outside in the cold, bright air, Sam kept Mac huddled close to his chest. "I'm going to carry you all the way!" he told his puppy.

Mac didn't seem to mind one bit. He rested his head against Sam's shoulder, watching the world go by as they walked. Amelia glanced up the hill towards the stables in the distance, and could just make out two dark shapes, racing backwards and forwards across the snow. *The reindeer!* she realised. *Jingle and Twinkle look like they're enjoying their Christmas, too!*

As Amelia looked back at the twinkling lights of the village, a huge flake of snow drifted past, brushing against her cheek. Then two more. A moment later the sky was full of

tumbling, feathery clumps.

"It's so beautiful," she said to Sam.

"It really is," he said, gazing out
over the snowy landscape. But then,
noticing they had stopped, Mac took
the opportunity to lick Sam's face again,
breathing steamy mist over him. Sam
leaned back, trying to escape Mac's
soggy tongue. "Let's get Mac home," he
said with a laugh. "I still need to give
him his present."

As they started off again, crunching
through the snow, Amelia let out a
contented sigh. *What a wonderful*
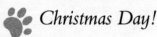 *Christmas Day!*

The End

Read on for a sneak peek at Amelia and Sam's next adventure!

ANIMAL ARK

Puppy Problem

Lucy Daniels

"This driveway goes on for ever!" Amelia Haywood said. She was walking through the grounds of Brambledown Hall with her mum and her best friend, Sam Baxter. The hall stood in the middle of its own estate, a large park on the outskirts of Welford village. There was green grass and trees as far as she could see. "Do you think we'll reach the hall before bedtime? Maybe we'll have to camp out with the deer!"

"That sounds awesome!" Sam said, his eyes shining.

Mum laughed, tucking a loose strand of hair behind her ear. "I'm afraid you won't need your pyjamas today. We're nearly there – look!" She pointed at the beautiful old building ahead.

Amelia grinned. *It's like a fairytale castle!* It was built of grey stone, with arched windows and pointed towers in the corners. She decided to bring a camera with her next time she came, so she could show Dad a photo. He lived in York and she was spending the second half of the summer holidays with him.

It was the first Saturday of the holidays now, and Mum was going to sign up for the annual Welford Gardening Contest. There was going to be a big launch party next weekend, and all the green-fingered villagers were getting ready to show off their gardens. Amelia was more interested in the creatures that lived in the woods around Brambledown Hall, though. *I really hope we see the deer today,* she thought excitedly.

"There!" Sam clutched Amelia's arm.

A cluster of reddish-brown animals grazed a short distance away. A couple lifted their heads to look at them, then turned back to nibbling at the grass.

Amelia's heart beat fast. "They're beautiful," she breathed.

A little fawn took a few steps towards them on long, skinny legs. He stumbled and another larger deer nudged him back again.

"Aw," said Amelia, shading her eyes to get a better view. "I wish we could get closer. But I read somewhere that it's not good for wild deer to get used to being around humans."

As they reached the entrance to the hall, Amelia noticed a poster about the Welford Gardening Contest fixed to the door. She read out some of the categories listed below: "Prettiest Borders, Best Hedge-cutting, Biggest Veg … Which one are you entering, Mum?"

"Well, the Biggest Veg contest is definitely out, seeing as slugs ate my cabbages." Mum frowned. "So I think I'm going for the Radiant Roses competition."

"You'll definitely win that one!" Amelia squeezed Mum's hand. "Your roses are so pretty!"

"Well, let's cross our fingers," Mum said, grinning.

"Just think, Mrs Haywood, if you win, your roses will be on the telly!" said Sam.

For the first time ever, the contest was being filmed for a gardening show called *Blooming Brilliant*. Amelia's gran was a big fan of the presenter, Bernard Bloom – and his pet dog, Pansy.

"Come on," said Amelia. "Let's have a look inside!"

They stepped through the hallway

into a big room that was full of tables and chairs, all piled up with pot plants, gardening twine, scissors and trowels. Villagers scurried about, carrying armfuls of flowers and vegetables.

As her mum went to sign up for the Radiant Roses competition, Amelia spotted Julia Kaminski, the receptionist at Animal Ark, sitting in her wheelchair next to a suit of armour. Another woman with long brown hair stood beside her, dressed in a blue hoodie, cutting up strips of ribbon to tie around bouquets. Julia looked up from the flowers she was arranging in a vase and waved at them.

"Hi, Julia!" Sam said.

"Hey there!" Julia replied. "This is my sister, Kasia. She's organising the contest this year." She nudged the woman beside her. "Kasia, this is Amelia and Sam – I told you about them, remember? They're our helpers at Animal Ark!"

Warmth swelled inside Amelia's chest. She was so proud of her role at the vet surgery.

"Lovely to meet you both!" Kasia said. "Isn't this amazing?" She gestured at the crowd, a smile breaking across her face.

"It's crazy in here!" said Sam. "I suppose everyone wants to win and get on TV."

"Is Bernard Bloom here yet?" Amelia

asked, hopefully. "My gran would love it if I could get his autograph for her."

"I'm afraid we've only got his picture so far." Kasia pointed to a cardboard cut-out behind her. It showed a man with twinkling blue eyes and floppy blond hair. He was holding Pansy, a Jack Russell cross terrier who wore a bandana made from the same spotty material as her owner's shirt. "We're expecting him tomorrow."

"He's going to be staying at our B&B," Sam told her proudly.

"Kasia, tell Amelia and Sam about Blossom!" Julia said, tying a red ribbon around her flowers.

Kasia grinned. "Blossom's my new cockapoo puppy. Would you like to meet her?"

"Yes, please!" Amelia's heart raced — she loved meeting new animals! *I've never seen a cockapoo before,* she thought. *I wonder what it will look like?*

Kasia turned towards a closed door. "I found her a quiet room so the kerfuffle out here doesn't unsettle her."

"Have you had her long?" Sam asked.

"Only a few days," Kasia said. "In her last home, the cat kept chasing her out of the house. She hid in the recycling box once and nearly got collected by the bin men!"

"You know, we could help train her," Amelia offered hopefully.

"We trained my Westie, Mac," added Sam. "And he was a real handful! Actually, he still is."

Kasia laughed. "That's kind of you. But Blossom's already trained! In fact, her last owner crate-trained her." She opened the door for them.

Amelia was about to ask what crate-training was, but she was distracted by the empty room. There was no sign of a puppy anywhere.

"Um, where is she?" Sam asked.

Kasia dashed in after them and gasped. "Blossom's gone!" She looked around, desperately. She darted over to the windows, checking they were all shut.

Worry spiked through Amelia's stomach. Where *had* Blossom gone?

And then she noticed a soft rumbling sound coming from a flowerpot in the corner. Amelia peered inside. She made out a pair of ears and a cute quivering nose amongst the bundle of curly black and white fur squeezed into the bottom of the pot. "Here she is!" she called. She lifted the warm, sleepy little puppy out.

"Thank goodness!" Kasia gasped. She took Blossom and cuddled her close, kissing her head. "You might be called Blossom, but that doesn't mean I can plant you in a pot and grow you!"

Blossom gave Kasia a big lick on the nose.

Kasia giggled. "Thanks, Amelia."

Amelia look back at the bustling hall and felt a squirm of anxiety. Kasia had adopted a puppy at a really busy time. Would Blossom need help to settle into Welford?

But Blossom's already been trained, she reasoned. *She should be fine… shouldn't she?*

Read **Puppy Problem** to find out what happens next …

Animal Advice

Do you love animals as much as Amelia and
Sam? Here are some tips on how to look after
them from veterinary surgeon Sarah McGurk.

Caring for your pet

1. Animals need clean water at all times.
2. They need to be fed too – ask your vet what kind of
   food is best, and how much the animal needs.
3. Some animals, such as dogs, need exercise every day.
4. Animals also need lots of love. You should always
   be very gentle with your pets and be careful not to do
   anything that might hurt them.

When to go to the vet

Sometimes animals get ill. Like you, they will mostly get better on their own. But if your pet has hurt itself or seems very unwell, then a trip to the vet might be needed. Some pets also need to be vaccinated, to prevent them from getting dangerous diseases. Your vet can tell you what your pet needs.

Helping wildlife

1 Always ask an adult before you go near any animals you don't know.

2 If you find an animal or bird which is injured or can't move, it is best not to touch it.

3 If you are worried, you can phone an animal charity such as the RSPCA (SSPCA in Scotland) for help.

Where animals need you!

www.animalark.co.uk